JESUS'
CHRISTMAS
PARTY

Nicholas Allan

A Doubleday Book for Young Readers

A Doubleday Book for Young Readers

Published by
Bantam Doubleday Dell Publishing Group, Inc.
1540 Broadway
New York, New York 10036

Doubleday and the portrayal of an anchor with a dolphin are trademarks of
Bantam Doubleday Dell Publishing Group, Inc.

Originally published in Great Britain by Hutchinson Children's Books,
Random House UK Limited 1991.

Library of Congress Cataloging-in-Publication Data

ISBN 0-385-32521-5
Cataloging-in-Publication Data is available from the U.S. Library of Congress.

Manufactured in China

November 1997

10 9 8 7 6 5 4 3 2

There was nothing
the innkeeper liked
more than a good
night's sleep.

But one night there was
a knock at the door.

"No room," said the innkeeper.
"But we're tired and have traveled
through night and day."
"There's only the stable around the back.
Here's two blankets. Sign the register."
So they signed it: "Mary and Joseph."

Then he shut the door,
climbed the stairs,
got into bed,
and went to sleep.

But then, later, there was
another knock at the door.

"Excuse me. I wonder if
you could lend us
another, smaller blanket?"

"There. One smaller blanket,"
said the innkeeper.

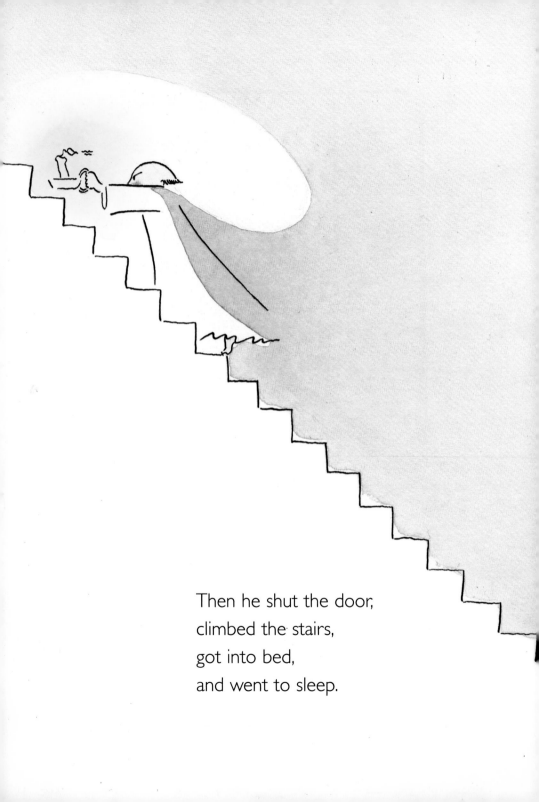

Then he shut the door,
climbed the stairs,
got into bed,
and went to sleep.

But then a bright light
woke him up.

"That's *all* I need,"
said the innkeeper.

Then he shut the door,
climbed the stairs,
drew the curtains,
got into bed,
and went to sleep.

But then there was *another*
knock at the door.

"We are three shepherds."

"Well, what's the matter? Lost your sheep?"

"We've come to see Mary and Joseph."

"AROUND THE BACK,"

said the innkeeper.

Then he shut the door,
climbed the stairs,
got into bed,
and went to sleep.

But then there was yet
another knock at the door.

"We are three kings. We've come—"

"AROUND THE BACK!"

He slammed the door,
climbed the stairs,
got into bed,
and went to sleep.

But *then* a chorus of
singing woke him up.

So he got out of bed,

stomped down the stairs,

threw open the door,

went around the back,

stormed into the stable, and was just about to speak when—

"Shhh!" whispered everybody.

"Baby?" said the innkeeper.

"Yes, a baby has this night been born."

"Oh?" said the innkeeper, looking
crossly into the manger.

And just at that moment, suddenly,
amazingly, his anger seemed to fly away.
"Oh," said the innkeeper, "isn't he *beautiful*!"

In fact, he thought the baby was so special .

so that they could com

. he woke up *all* the guests at the inn,

ıd look at the baby too.

No one got much sleep that night!

THE END